8/26/80

Swan Lake

Swan Lake

ADAPTED AND ILLUSTRATED BY

Donna Diamond

INTRODUCTION BY

Clive Barnes

HOLIDAY HOUSE · NEW YORK

For Judes and Stephen, with love

Copyright © 1980 by Donna Diamond
Introduction copyright © 1980 by Clive Barnes
All rights reserved
Printed in the United States of America

Library of Congress Cataloging in Publication Data

Diamond, Donna.
Swan Lake.

SUMMARY: A prince's love for a swan queen is
thwarted by an evil sorcerer in this fairy tale
adaptation of the classic ballet.
1. Chaikovskii, Petr Il'ich, 1840-1893. The
swan lake—Juvenile literature.   [1. Chaikovskii,
Petr Il'ich, 1840-1893. The swan lake.
2. Ballets—Stories, plots, etc. 3. Fairy tales]
I. Title
GV1790.S8D5   792.8'4   79-11179
ISBN 0-8234-0356-4

This story adaptation of the classical ballet, Swan Lake, is based on
the original book by V. P. Begitchev and Vasily Geltzer (1877) and
the Marius Petipa-Lev Ivanov version (1895). It was first performed
at the Bolshoi Theatre, Moscow, March 4, 1877, with music by Peter
Ilyich Tchaikovsky, and with Pauline Karpakova dancing the leading
role. Later it was staged at the Maryinsky Theatre, St. Petersburg,
January 17, 1895, with Pierina Legnani in the double role of Odette-
Odile. An abridged version of Swan Lake was first presented in the
U.S.A. at the Metropolitan Opera House, New York, December 20,
1911. Catherine Geltzer danced the role of Odette-Odile and Mikhail
Mordkin performed as Prince Siegfried.

Of all the ballets that have entered the international repertory,
Swan Lake has possessed the most mysterious allure. Its Tchaikovsky
music is possibly unequaled among the ballet classics in its range and
appeal. The standard version of the choreography remains a yardstick
of ballet excellence, as does the mythical magic, the fairytale romance
of the story.

The simple symbolism of good and evil makes a basic appeal to
mankind. The ballet represents heroism and love. It also represents
tragedy because of the hero's failure to realize his true destiny.

This picture version of the story fascinates me partly because of the
simple, charming, yet explicit images of Odette and Siegfried and their
tragic love. But also because it creates some special evocation for
children of the ballet itself.

In the nineteenth century, certain lithographs of famous ballets were
produced, and sometimes they were called by that admirably old-
fashioned name, "a keepsake." This book also is a wonderful keepsake of that great ballet called Swan Lake.

CLIVE BARNES

nce upon a time, in a kingdom far away, there lived a Princess Mother and her son, Siegfried. On the Prince's twenty-first birthday, his friends gathered in the royal garden. They celebrated his coming of age among lanterns and pennants, irises and roses. Wolfgang, the Prince's old tutor, doddered about while Benno, the Prince's closest friend, stood beside a peach tree.

The guests were merry and, as afternoon turned to dusk, the gaiety grew. Wolfgang refilled his goblet with wine and danced a jig on unsteady legs. As candles were lit around the garden, a messenger appeared.

"The Princess Mother would like an audience with the Prince," the messenger said.

Wolfgang wobbled to a stop. The guests fell silent. The old tutor was wiping some wine from his beard as the Princess Mother entered. She was surrounded by pages and ladies-in-waiting.

Prince Siegfried walked to his mother's side and kissed her hand. "Good evening, Mother," he said. The guests stepped back nervously as he escorted her to the center of the garden.

"I see you are aware this evening marks your coming of age," the Princess Mother said. "But now I expect you to assume the responsibilities of your title. I wish you to marry, and a suitable wife must be found." The guests began to murmur as she continued. "I have arranged a ball for tomorrow night where you will choose a bride from the loveliest noblewomen in the land.''

The Prince did not answer. The idea of marrying upset him. The Princess Mother said good-night, gathered her long train and, followed by her entourage, left the garden.

The moon, like a circle of ice, rose in the night sky. With goblets of sweet red wine, the guests toasted the Prince, and again the garden was filled with laughter and dancing. But the Prince was moody. He did not wish to marry. A flock of wild swans flew across the sky, and he watched them restlessly.

"Benno," the Prince called. "Bring me my crossbow."

Benno looked up. "What, a hunt at this hour?"

The Prince clapped his friend on the shoulder. "Come, gather a hunting party to follow the wild swans."

Wolfgang protested. "Nay, do not heed him. The hour is late, and it is time to retire."

But the young men were already gathering their bows. Prince Siegfried beckoned them into the woods, leaving Wolfgang behind, alone beneath the lanterns.

The hunting party wandered in the forest, cutting paths through the dark leaves. The men searched for the shape of swans in the sky. Soon they came to a lake, as smooth as silver in the moonlight. Beside it were the ruins of an old cathedral. Hidden among the stones and shadows was a flock of wild swans. Their wings pulsed gently, and the moonlight seemed to sleep upon their feathers. The men paused.

Prince Siegfried stared at the mysterious birds. He signaled his friends to put down their bows. Then he walked toward the old cathedral. In a few moments he was deep within the temple of ancient stones.

Suddenly a girl appeared before him. She was very beautiful. A crown of jewels and feathers rested upon her head, and a scented mist enclosed her. She backed away from the Prince.

"I will not hurt you," he said.

But the girl was afraid. She fluttered like a bird, and her eyes never left the crossbow in Prince Siegfried's hand.

"I will not hurt you," he said again, as he placed the crossbow on the ground beside him.

The girl's trembling quieted. But the Prince could see

she was still afraid. For a while he did not say anything. "Who are you?" he finally asked.

The girl touched the crown upon her head. "I am Odette, Queen of the Swans," she said. Her voice was as delicate as the sound of silk. But it was also sad. "When I was a child, Von Rothbart, an evil sorcerer, stole me from my mother. He turned me into a swan and called me Queen. I live my days as a swan, and at night, between midnight and dawn, I am human." Then she added, "Nights pass quickly, and daybreak is always sad."

Prince Siegfried felt deeply stirred. He wanted to touch her. "Odette, how can you be freed from this spell?"

Her reply came slowly, as if the words were difficult to say. "I will always be a swan, unless a man pledges to love me, marry me, and never love another."

Siegfried watched Odette as her fingers traced the patterns of moonlight on the crumbling stone. Suddenly he understood that he loved her. Reaching out, he touched a strand of hair that fell across her cheek. "I love you," he said. Odette did not answer. "Tomorrow night there is a ball," he continued. "You must come. I will pledge my love to you before everyone at court."

But again Odette did not answer. Instead she wrapped her arms around his shoulders. For a moment her happiness was as visible as the sun. Then she backed away.

"We cannot be together," she said. "Von Rothbart is very strong. He will keep us apart."

"I love you," Siegfried said again.

"Von Rothbart will not let me go to the ball," she insisted. "He will use his power against us."

"I love you," the Prince repeated once more.

"There is great danger!" she cried.

The Prince took her in his arms. "I will break this spell. I will love you forever. I will . . ." He did not know what to say.

Dawn was coming. Odette trembled. The shadows began to dissolve in the morning light. Odette shivered. Now Prince Siegfried dared not speak. He too sensed something that he could not control. From behind the stones, he heard a soft rustling. Slowly a young girl emerged. Another appeared beside her and then another. The Prince remembered the mysterious swans as he watched the maidens gather in the mist. Their bodies pulsed, bound in a strange rhythm. Siegfried held Odette tighter, but he felt her quiver and pull away.

"What is happening?" Siegfried demanded.

As the hoot of an owl echoed through the ruins, Odette replied, "Von Rothbart calls us."

"Do not leave me," Siegfried pleaded.

But Odette backed away from the Prince, and the maidens encircled her. "There is great danger." Her voice scarcely wrinkled the air.

"I love you," the Prince called to her. But she had vanished.

Prince Siegfried ran out of the cathedral and found his friends asleep on the bank of the lake. The morning sky was the color of a peach. "Have you seen her?" Siegfried cried.

Benno rubbed his eyes. "I do not understand, my Lord. Whom do you mean?"

The hoot of an owl floated over the lake on the wind. The Prince pointed to the sky. In the distance, a flock of swans was flying away.

Benno stood beside the Prince. "What has happened, my Lord?"

Siegfried searched the sky. The swans had disappeared into the horizon.

"I am tired. Let us head for home," was all he said.

On the evening of the ball, Prince Siegfried wandered through the corridors of the castle. He imagined he was still in the dark cathedral by the lake, but the sound of footsteps interrupted his secret thoughts. He saw Benno walking quickly toward him.

"Make haste, my Lord, the guests are arriving," Benno said.

Prince Siegfried showed no enthusiasm. He did not want to go to the ball, but he nodded and smoothed his velvet doublet.

In the great hall of the castle, the guests were gathered like a display of royal jewels. Ambassadors, drinking from golden goblets, mingled in groups while ladies rustled past. Wolfgang chattered happily but stopped and bowed when he saw the Prince. Siegfried returned the bow but only glanced at the guests.

Within moments, the sound of a trumpet heralded the arrival of the Princess Mother. Followed by her cortege, she walked across the hall to the Prince and kissed him. He returned her kiss listlessly.

"Are you ill?" she asked.

"No, Mother," Siegfried reassured her.

"Then you must pay more attention to our guests or they will remark upon your behavior." And, with a regal gesture, she summoned six young women to stand before her. One by one she presented them to her son.

The first had an ivory complexion.

The second wore a gown of silver brocade.

The third had azure eyes.

The fourth carried a fan of turquoise feathers.

The fifth had flame-colored curls.

And the sixth smiled like a child.

But none of them could compare to Prince Siegfried's memory of Odette. He turned away.

Bewildered, the Princess Mother conferred with Wolfgang. "In your opinion, who among these noblewomen has produced a favorable impression upon the Prince?"

"So far," Wolfgang replied, "there seems to be no one who appeals to him, your Majesty."

The Princess Mother shrugged her shoulders and signaled to the musicians. Under her watchful eye, Siegfried danced in turn with the six young women. But after each dance he escorted his partner back to his mother as if returning an unread book to a shelf.

He thought of Odette's warning. "There is great danger." The Prince repeated her words quietly. He drifted to a window and looked out at the dark, distant edge of the woods. He cooled his forehead against the glass as the moon stirred his memory.

Suddenly a page announced the arrival of an unknown baron and his daughter, Odile. Siegfried turned from the window. He saw a tall, bearded man enter the great hall with a woman in a night-black gown. As the Prince walked toward them, he caught the sweet scent of the evening forest. He was struck by the way Odile held her head, the curve of her neck, the whiteness of her skin. He felt he was looking at Odette.

The Prince presented himself to the Baron and his daughter. "Odile, is it possible we have met before?" Siegfried asked.

"No, my Lord," she replied. "We are seeing each other for the first time." As Odile spoke, it was Odette whom he heard. As he gazed at Odile's face, it was Odette whom he recognized. The Prince looked into her eyes. They were as cold as crystal but he saw only their brightness.

Bowing to his mother and then the Baron, Siegfried led Odile across the floor. The whole court looked on as he paused, studying her face as if to draw it. Then he took her in his arms, and they began to dance. Slowly, at first, they glided to the center of the hall. The tiers of Odile's skirt brushed the guests. The chorus of instruments and voices swelled, and the Prince held Odile closer.

As the dance ended, the guests burst into applause. Wolfgang pounded the floor with his cane, and the Princess Mother smiled at the Baron.

But Siegfried and Odile did not leave the floor. The

Prince reached out and touched a strand of hair that fell across Odile's cheek. "I love you," he whispered.

Suddenly a swan appeared at the window. A crown of jewels and feathers rested upon its head. Odile stepped quickly between the Prince and the trembling silhouette. "What do you mean?" she asked. The swan's wings beat against the panes of glass.

"I want to marry you," Siegfried said.

"And you will never love another?" she urged.

Siegfried took her hands and bent to kiss their open palms. But he was interrupted by the Princess Mother.

"My son, you may not kiss a lady's hand unless you are betrothed."

"I am willing to pledge my love," the Prince declared. "I will love her, marry her, and never love another."

At that moment, the room darkened. A violent wind blew through the great hall, shattering windowpanes and scattering broken glass upon the floor. Now Siegfried saw the swan floating in the cracked window. Suddenly the Prince understood. His love had been misplaced. Odile was not Odette, and the unknown baron was Von Rothbart.

"Odette," the Prince cried, "I have been deceived!"

The swan dissolved like smoke into the night air. Siegfried turned toward the Baron, but the Baron had changed. A huge winged creature with an enormous, plumed head stood by Odile's side.

Siegfried fled. Behind him, the great hall echoed with Von Rothbart's hideous laughter.

The Prince ran through the woods toward the lake. The moon had disappeared behind the clouds, and the forest paths were hidden in darkness.

When he reached the lake, he saw the swan maidens, like scattered pearls, along the shore. Their bodies beat from side to side, and the wind whipped their hair about their shoulders. In the distance, the Prince heard thunder. The ancient cathedral crouched beside the lake. Amid the stones of the ruins, Siegfried saw Odette. He called her name, but she did not answer. He ran to her and clasped her shoulders. "Odette," the Prince pleaded, "forgive me."

"You have betrayed me," she cried. "You have pledged your love to another." The sound of thunder was nearer now, and lightning streaked the sky. "Von Rothbart has won." Her words could barely be heard above the wind. "Now only in death will I be released from his spell." Her voice broke.

Siegfried was silent. He could not answer because he was crying. For a long time, they held each other without speaking.

The hoot of an owl floated through the ruins. "Let me go on by myself," Odette said.

She began to climb the crumbling stones of the cathedral. When she had reached the highest stone, she steadied herself. She stood there for only a moment. Then she stepped forward. Odette fell into the lake as gently as a feather falls.

Siegfried ran to the bank and lunged into the angry water. At first, he was tossed by the waves. Then he disappeared. The maidens watched the surface of the lake for a long time. The thunder faded, and the water grew calm.

As the first sign of dawn touched the sky with violet, the maidens heard the hoot of an owl. Von Rothbart was calling them. Their bodies pressed together. Again the maidens heard the low, hollow call. They shivered. In the mist of daybreak, they vanished.

Through the night, men from the court had wandered in search of Siegfried. They came upon the lake at sunrise. It was very still. The men stood in the morning shadows and heard the hoot of an owl.

Benno pointed to the sky. "Look," he said. In the distance, a flock of wild swans was flying away.

For many days, Benno and the men searched for the Prince. But Siegfried was never found.